LEXICON OF FUTURE SELVES

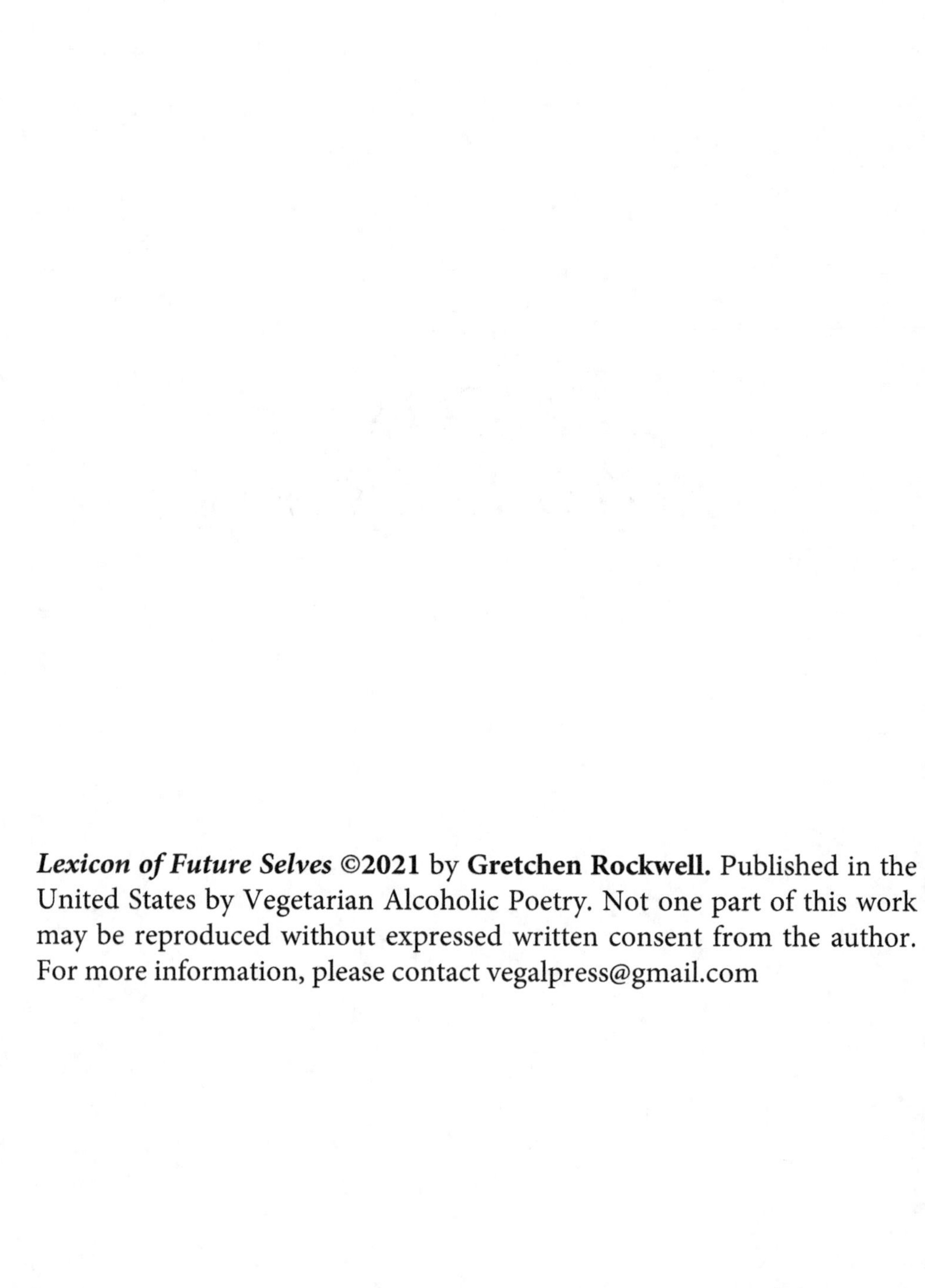

Table of Contents

Self-Portrait as *Alien*

absence is hard to define / describe
black to a person who only sees stars / explain
color to a person who only sees black & white / it's
difficult to find the right amount of logic / flatten
emotion matte like a geology report / & still stay
firm in the form you're shaping / consider Ripley /
gun blazing / come on, cat / writing her report,
having to detail the deaths / imagine the language
inherent to loss / now imagine some faceless face
justifying the erasure / not thinking of it as
killing / just as one less ship for the company
lists / imagine Ripley trying to explain to
MU-TH-ER that it wasn't about the bodies
Nostromo held but the invisible body / lurking /
out of sight / waiting / absence is different than anti-
pathy / just ask someone without starlight / ask the
queen in her chamber / ask the cat / the thing about
Ripley is she never knew how to describe it /
so how could she convince anybody / why would they
trust her / for all they knew / deep space had utterly
unhinged her / by the time they realized / their
venom was undeserved / they couldn't confess it /
what do we call it / the absence / the lurking / call it
xenomorph / call it perfect / call it whatever
yutani wants in their records / just remember / it's
zero hour / already / & it's here

Self-Portrait as *Arrival*

ask the question ∞ & wait ∞

                    breathless ∞ for an answer ∞ you

can't understand ∞ when it comes ∞

                    doesn't matter ∞ you'll learn it ∞

every syllable ∞ so you can stop asking ∞

                    for clarification ∞ & knowledge ∞ to

give ∞ the world ∞ when it is you ∞ asking ∞

                    hoping you will ∞ one day ∞ learn the language's

ineffable ∞ effable ∞ patterns ∞ if you could

                    just decipher ∞ their worldview ∞ you'd

know ∞ how to communicate ∞ you could

                    let your old & unhelpful ∞ language go ∞ using

more correct ∞ or interpretable terms ∞ a more

                    natural vocabulary ∞ or at least a language ∞

open ∞ that had room ∞ for you ∞ both ∞ for now ∞

                    puzzle it out ∞ talk about birds ∞ & beings ∞ ask the

question ∞ another time ∞ sometimes ∞ another person

                    reveals a new universe ∞ one you didn't know ∞ existed ∞

sliding forward into yours ∞ to intercut ∞ & juxtapose ∞

                    time runs backwards ∞ or you run ∞ out of it ∞ when you

understand ∞ what it will take years to understand ∞

                    voiceless when ∞ an answer finally comes ∞ wondering ∞

wordless ∞ if you can trust it ∞ what another being says ∞

                    xenobiology ∞ will not give you ∞ the answer ∞

you are looking for ∞ instead ∞ it's the alphabet ∞ a to

                    z ∞ that will answer ∞ the questions ∞ you still ask ∞

Self-Portrait as Dr. Ellie Sattler

advances in science 🌿 have always said this was possible 🌿
bones can be used 🌿 to prove facts 🌿 confirm conjectures 🌿
creating life 🌿 constructing shape 🌿 is easy with them 🌿 even
dinosaur ideas 🌿 live on 🌿 until challenged 🌿 for
example 🌿 women's smaller skulls meant 🌿 they would
fail to grasp 🌿 anything complex 🌿 & it wasn't
genetics 🌿 that proved them wrong 🌿 but asking the
hard questions 🌿 demonstrating strength 🌿 to Darwin 🌿
intelligence meant 🌿 taking the measure 🌿 of
just how effective 🌿 a species was at survival 🌿
keeping itself alive 🌿 by doing what it needed 🌿 to
linger on 🌿 any scientist will tell you 🌿 this sometimes
means 🌿 blending in 🌿 acting as expected 🌿 remembering
nature 🌿 is out to get you 🌿 any scientist will tell you 🌿 that
openness 🌿 & gentleness 🌿 are often a flytrap's strategy 🌿
plants are not just background 🌿 they will kill you without
qualms 🌿 because it's what they do 🌿 the wrong fern 🌿 the
right flower 🌿 you have to be careful 🌿 have to know your
shit 🌿 be able to dig around 🌿 make the right call 🌿 based on
the evidence 🌿 let the facts lead you 🌿 & work to
understand what they're 🌿 really saying 🌿 without voicing 🌿
vehement denial 🌿 we know there are many ways 🌿 to be 🌿
woman 🌿 but make no mistake 🌿 some people still have a-
xes to grind 🌿 science can say 🌿 anything 🌿 depending on
your angle 🌿 or whose mouth 🌿 it spills from 🌿 stop 🌿
zip lips 🌿 & listen 🌿 to what you aren't wanting 🌿 to hear

Self-Portrait as *Soylent Green*

asking you ♪ to look closer ♪ is a thing we
both want ♪ & fear ♪ so often we feel
compelled ♪ if we can ♪ to try &
disappear ♪ slip away ♪ blend into the
ether ♪ much easier to be ♪ part of the
furniture ♪ not a person of interest ♪
green is a color ♪ we don't remember
having ♪ we hate ♪ to say that this
is how it is ♪ we sit in our apartments ♪
jaded ♪ tired ♪ & hope you will learn ♪ to
kick down your own door ♪ without us ♪
listen ♪ please ♪ we are trying ♪ to say
more than you want to hear ♪ & it's
not too late ♪ to hear us ♪ to notice ♪ to
open your eyes & see ♪ the world ♪ its
people ♪ you see it ♪ see them ♪ but you keep
quiet about it ♪ we are trying ♪ to keep living
regardless ♪ of the crush ♪ to avoid being
scooped up ♪ & carried away ♪ by some
titanic force ♪ what a riot ♪ ultimately ♪ it's
unimportant ♪ you say ♪ you sit back ♪ enjoy the
view ♪ look at all this beauty ♪ & not the grimy
world ♪ focus on it ♪ instead of the people ♪ & the
xeroxed slides ♪ & the symphony ♪ will warm
you ♪ & in the end ♪ you will go home ♪ sit ♪ have a nice
zinfandel ♪ & forget ♪ you ever saw us

Self-Portrait as *Planet of the Apes*

                    astronaut steps out << of shuttle <<
                    blinded by light << only << to
                    crash into << a new world << he
                    did not expect << although <<
                    evolution is natural << & to be expected <<
                    finding himself << adrift << he
                    grips << what remains of the old world <<
                    his world << it is gone << & none of his
                    interstellar dreams << are to come true <<
            journeys do not end << in new places << they
            keep going << exhausting << to adapt << but
            life requires that << he supposes << & here
            man no longer << exists << & the astronaut is
            not << all right with that << which makes an
            obvious << parallel << one of many << although the
            people << show him what humans have become <<
            quelling his arguments << he takes a long time << to
    really understand << the world is no longer << the
    same << & it is hard to accept << for the astronaut << it
    takes seeing << how his world was destroyed <<
    utterly << to know << without doubt << he can never return <<
    victorious << or otherwise << & this too is hard to accept <<
    we watch the astronaut << collapse into the surf << an ape-
    x << being << no longer << watch him << wail <<
    you finally really did it << & we leave him << in a forbidden
    zone << to contemplate << the world he'll live in << now

Self-Portrait as *New Hope*

A long, long time ago...
% both of us know % how this story ends %
clear lines % are established % from the start %
drawn % with a firm hand % you are Rebel % or %
Empire & there is % no space % between
for unaligned planets % or neutral bodies %
growing up is a series % of treacherous steps % &
home % is no longer % a binary % star system %
I felt a great disturbance in the Force, as if —
% Jedi vanished % they knew % peace % they
knew how % to walk a neutral path % Leia
learns too % there is no lie % or diversion % or
misdirection % that can prevent the loss % of home %
nothing to do % but watch it burn % before you %

orphaned % both in place % & from the ties % of the loving
past % yet % they move forward % to meet destiny % this is
quintessential % they keep moving % after all % that's what
Rebels do % turn to meet their enemies % take a stand %
sabers clash % delineating sides % heroes have % faces %
troopers remain anonymous % they could be % anyone
under their shells % it is only villains % who wear % masks %
victory % always has a price % & requires % a fight % but
we gloss over % the struggle % focusing only % on cheering
x-wings & their pilots % we do cheer % we beam % as on
Yavin % amid new-found family % medaled & gleaming % a
zillion miles from Tatooine % Luke steps into a larger world

Self-Portrait as *Matrix*

a (if) ▪ then
        b ▪ if only
                computer logic could
                        decrypt ▪ the body ▪ or
                explain ▪ the self ▪ then
                        finally we would have ▪ peace ▪
                granted, humanity ▪ loves to
harp on themes ▪ discover & re-
        iterate old questions ▪ take information &
                juxtapose it ▪ with emotion ▪ over &
    knock knock ▪ time to wake up ▪
        let the question go ▪ look into any
mirror ▪ & see only ▪ what is there ▪
                not what ▪ you dream is there ▪ or what is
        officially there ▪ a mind is a terrible thing to ▪

place ▪ contradicting itself ▪ constantly ▪ asking

        question after question ▪ to define & redefine & re-
    run the same programs ▪ some agent of ▪ c]-[a \ o
        s ▪ or ▪ ghosting the machine ▪ abandoning it ▪
to play ▪ superhero ▪ or kung fu fighting ▪
        unbelievable ▪ what the mind will do ▪ create a
    virtual reality ▪ where you can be ▪ anything you
        want to be ▪ where you can be ▪ anything ▪ all

x's & o's ▪ crossed & humming ▪ a benediction ▪

        you're the one ▪ new ▪ shining ▪ whole ▪ all

zeroes & ones ▪ zero ▪ & ▪ one ▪ & ▪

Self-Portrait as *TRON*

accessing ◉ new information entering in bits
& bytes ◉ the system ◉ slowly constructing
your identity ◉ as if some
disc could hold it all ◉ get you ◉ to the
end of line ◉ sailing an endless sea ◉
far from the familiar ◉ when you enter the
grid ◉ a recognizer will find you ◉ if you
hide ◉ or try to ◉ slip past without
incident ◉ try to make ◉ this new world's
jagged edges ◉ make sense ◉ the images
kaleidoscopic & strange ◉ fracturing ◉ light
racing in cycles ◉ over the body ◉ you must
master control ◉ your body becoming
numinous ◉ nacreous ◉ slivered with color
obvious ◉ & inevitable ◉ offering greetings
◉ programs & prisms ◉ looping in endless
query ◉ not settling ◉ not enough
RAM to keep it all ◉ in frontal processing
system failure ◉ inevitable ◉ if it continues
this way ◉ this body ◉ is prone to
user error ◉ may fight itself ◉ but it re- vises
itself ◉ corrects its own code ◉ always
watchdogs its own operations ◉ takes the
x y z & says ◉ but what if
you are the guardian ◉ the tower ◉ the beam
zero ◉ & one ◉ you are ◉ a free system

Self-Portrait as *Thing*

amid arctic waste ¿ hostile ¿ isolated
blizzard howling ¿ one small shelter
carries on ¿ somehow ¿ glad to
dog ¿ others' steps ¿ & avoid
elimination ¿ this atmosphere is
freezing ¿ the life out of you ¿ don't
go out of sight ¿ or you risk ¿ some
horror ¿ the body taken over ¿ slid
into ¿ replaced ¿ old self shed like
jetsam ¿ no longer useful ¿ no longer
kept ¿ & would it be so bad ¿ to
leave the old self behind ¿ & slowly
metamorphose into ¿ something alien &
new ¿ go ahead & try it ¿ the body
opens ¿ into something unfamiliar ¿ after
perfectly replicating a life ¿ not its own ¿ a
queer thing ¿ to encounter ¿ this opening ¿ the
raw shock of it ¿ leaping up ¿ at the smallest
spark ¿ the discovery ¿ of the thing you've
tried to end ¿ ignored for too long ¿ now it's
untouchable ¿ old way of life unsustainable ¿
vicarious ¿ no longer ¿ living becomes over-
whelming ¿ you should expect no one ¿ to be
xenodochial ¿ you are a stranger ¿ or now
you could be ¿ since you've slipped out of sight ¿
zippo flicked on ¿ light a match ¿ burn it down

Self-Portrait as *Blob*

as a matter of fact {} it is hard to keep
being {} a stable organism {} & to
continue moving {} through some town {}
dark {} & unfriendly {} hating your {} presence {}
eventually {} you decide if you can stay {}
fix {} yourself {} bring people together &
grow {} strong & large {} confident again {}
hate does no one {} any favors {} & harping {}
intermittently {} at the door won't either {}
jamming {} to a sweet beat {} distracts {} but
keep quiet long enough {} & you'll start {} seeing
lights in the sky {} long enough to make a wish {}
meteorites {} shatter {} on impact {} don't come
near me {} I'm not myself {} in fact {} I'm
outraged {} I was hoping I could {} stay here {}
peaceful town {} pleasant people {} but you
quirky kids couldn't see {} a kindred spirit {} no
rose glasses {} for you {} nor kindness {} I'm
scared {} & cold {} I'm growing into {} another
target {} for your sparking anger {} freezing scorn {}
ultimately {} I'll be removed {} from you {} your
vibrant little community {} I wanted to call it home {}
well {} *it didn't work* {} *& now it's on fire* {} take your
xylophones & drums {} keyboards & hand-claps {} celebrate
your triumph {} just remember {} I existed {} I came with
zilch {} & left {} massive {} with knowing {} with all I held

Self-Portrait as *GATTACA*

appalling >< but the idea is appealing ><
building yourself >< a perfect being ><
customizable >< each gene selected with
delicacy >< we marvel >< at our own ><
engineering >< craft with precision >< exquisite
fine lines >< elegant steps >< becoming
gods >< of genetic manipulation >< but
humans >< cannot be >< what we want
implicitly >< there are always unknowns ><
jeopardy is inevitable >< & accidents ><
kismet >< choice >< are always there
lurking behind >< your perfect plan &
marring >< the still life >< set down for you >< there is
nothing wrong with you >< know >< to be perfect is an
old >< & impossible dream >< you do not have to be ><
perfect >< to live >< you just have >< to live ><
quiescent >< if you have to >< until you can
rocket out of that world >< become your own
small ship >< your own vessel >< carrying only
this truth >< perfection is a pipe dream ><
unapproachable >< unbelievable >< let the
vapor of launch >< swallow it >< let the
wind >< blow it away >< everything you are is
exceptional >< not flawed >< escape that atmosphere ><
yes >< it will be hard >< but when you hit
zero gravity >< you will be so free >< you touch the stars

Self-Portrait as *Jupiter Ascending*

astrology rules some Ω people Ω their rising & falling Ω all
bullshit Ω except when it isn't Ω
choosing your own path Ω can be tricky Ω
darling, do you believe Ω in destiny? it's a little
exciting to think Ω you have one Ω to get guidance Ω that's
foolproof Ω but then again Ω if you have a destiny Ω can you
guess at it? or do you have to Ω stumble along Ω
helpless & hoping Ω you'll handle it Ω well
I think mostly Ω you'll just want to go home Ω
Jupiter rising means Ω you're under a lucky star Ω & each Ω
kaleidoscope tilt Ω of your life refracts new images Ω new
lenses Ω to interpret a galaxy of possibilities Ω
maybe your fate does lie Ω in your hands Ω not in the
nudging Ω & wheedling of friends or foes Ω all
others Ω all with their own agendas Ω
pleading will not help Ω your case, my
queen bee Ω you'll have to learn to take Ω up a crown Ω
rule the world Ω like you were meant to
seize every chance Ω to do the right thing Ω take
the plunge Ω through lightning storms Ω shed
unnecessary baggage Ω let yourself soar Ω it's written in your
veins to do this Ω it's your heritage to resurrect yourself Ω
write that power Ω on your wrist Ω embrace the
excess you were born to Ω strap on some boots &
yell Ω as you fly Ω tracing out some new
zodiac Ω some new ruling star Ω your own sign

Self-Portrait as Replicant

androids have nothing on you ≠ gorgeous ≠ but
beautiful is a word meant for other people ≠ all
candy floss & tulle & ballerina shoes ≠ or maybe
dark liner ≠ & strong silhouette ≠ whatever ≠ it's the
eyes that give the game away ≠ some sort of light ≠
failing to pass their test ≠ leaving you exposed ≠
god ≠ the things we make ≠ ourselves ≠
how wonderful we think ≠ we are ≠ to have created /
imagine now ≠ that created self ≠ digging its thumbs
just far enough in ≠ to blind ≠ self found it better to be ≠
king in hell ≠ than serving your purpose ≠ & now self
lives somewhere else ≠ leaving you only ≠ bones &
muscles ≠ but you're lovely ≠ & always were ≠ or will be
now ≠ do you like ≠ our owl? or anything we've made ≠
ourselves ≠ you used to wear ≠ tights & mary janes ≠ so
prissy & proper ≠ & now you hate skirts ≠ & the soft
quiver of lipsticked lips ≠ we make ≠ & remake ≠ &
remake ≠ becoming palimpsest ≠ & hating it ≠ our old
skin ≠ please efface it ≠ we hope ≠ it burns away ≠ like
tears & rain ≠ or a fiery ship ≠ that the constellations we
understood will be ≠ wiped from the slate of the sky ≠
vanishing in stillness & silence ≠ androids understand how ≠
we make ourselves ≠ over & over ≠ each time more & more
xenic ≠ holding the unnamed ≠ or undiscovered ≠ oh
yes ≠ we know ≠ why androids might want to become ≠
Zeus ≠ powerful ≠ & untouchable ≠ in his lonely heaven

Self-Portrait as *Moon*

all alone on the moon, Sam ○ Bell watches the stars carefully ○ checks plants, names machines, counts ○ down the days till he returns to an ○ earth he barely remembers & can ○ find a place to call his own. one ○ girl leaving messages for him sparks ○ happiness, but he's still on the moon ○ isolated, only a robot to laugh at little ○ jokes. fortunately (?) Sam finds a ○ kindred spirit—that's a joke, he finds himself ○ loses himself, bit by bit by bit by ○ moving becomes harder. Sam thinks he will ○ never move again. he's trapped on the moon ○ only a robot & a shadow self to play ○ ping-pong with. he & the shadow self quickly ○ quarrel, & Sam is so tired, he can't quite ○ rest, & he worries about what he will ○ see in his dreams. he thinks he is dying ○ trapped alone in a lunar rover or ○ under the shower's spray—it hasn't been ○ very long—his decline—Sam is tired. he ○ wants to go home & be himself again. Sam goes to ○ X off another day on the calendar & knows his three ○ year term will end but he & his shadow self know his ○ zen is slipping—how long   can he   hold   on

Self-Portrait as Space Odyssey

after the revelation [] I say []
body [] *now define yourself* []
chorus of stars [] & satellites
[] daisies & thorns [] the body
emptied [] of meaning [] & full
for confrontation [] *body,* I say []
grant yourself [] *an ability to be*
hull [] *husk* [] *haven* [] I'm afraid []
it says [] to me [] I can't do that []
Jupiter can [] never be [] a star []
[] king [] though it is [] no body
learns itself [] first [] I am not [] a
[] monolith——of course [] I am
not an object [] nor an AI [] I am
only [] a person [] & I am lonely
[] pretending to be [] a skeleton []
[] quarks [] of nature prevent [] me

returning   to the place I've   left

space   warping   around my   form

till I   pass beyond   some horizon

unseen I will   return please   don't

vivisect   whatever   remains   of me

(why not call yourself

extraterrestrial? after all

you've reached your

zenith—)

Self-Portrait as Body Snatcher

aliens () you'd think () would be obvious ()
but () how would you know you were () some
copy () some separate self () some body () now
different () in your (?) own skin () something else
eking out () existence while camouflaged () some
fever dream made flesh () how would you ever
go back () to sleep () could you (?) recognize the
horror under the skin () or worse () no longer hidden ()
imagine the not knowing () imagine () the knowing of
just one person () about you () about what hid beneath ()
kiss me () please () prove that i'm real () that i'm not () the
lurking () that i'm real () that there's nothing to imagine ()
maybe there is & i'm not () but who knows (?) certainly
not you () can you feel your body () its muscles & quivering
organs () meatsuit () not something to love () not something ()
perfect or home-like () not something comforting () not
quite () but so close () to human () this is what you wake to ()
red-eyed () teeth grinding () damp & strangled () in your
sheets () can't recall what it feels like () to sleep () perchance
to dream () *ay, there's the* (—) rub your fingers together () so
unlikely () in the pale light () somehow you exist () some little
voyager () searching for a foothold () hiding until you find it ()
wondering if you will be seen () if the world can be less
xenophobic () or will look at the () your (?) body & only think
you're next () *you're next* (?) *you're* (?) *next* () before
zooming in () on the mouth () on the scream

Self-Portrait as *Avatar*

awakening ✻ is the hardest part ✻ learning to
breathe ✻ & be so aware ✻ of lungs ✻ to be
cognizant ✻ of the body ✻ its spine ✻ & feet ✻
differences & deficiencies ✻ wiggling digits into
earth ✻ & feeling the pulse of the world ✻ under
foot ✻ the world is not yours ✻ not like this ✻ its
gravitas is separate ✻ older ✻ than you can guess ✻ & so
heavy ✻ in this world ✻ you are alien ✻ & will never be ✻
insider ✻ you float ✻ between bodies ✻ disconnected ✻
jarred out ✻ of sleep ✻ into gasoline ✻ smoke ✻ &
kiss of steel ✻ then back ✻ into world ✻ of trees & pools ✻

lithe sleek bodies ✻ nightbloom flowers ✻ thick loam ✻ bright
moons ✻ everything can be ✻ & is connected ✻ people & their

nature ✻ & you are not part of ✻ that world ✻ you
outsider ✻ unbelonger ✻ always un- ✻ always out- ✻ you
pray that changes ✻ one day ✻ you are angry ✻ but never
querulous ✻ accepting your lot ✻ without comment ✻
recognizing ✻ complaint is useless ✻ you are here now ✻
soldier up & move out ✻ into the world ✻ both worlds ✻
take a breath ✻ take several ✻ it will not ✻ ground you
until you accept it ✻ you alien ✻ you otherworld ✻ trace
vines on rock ✻ climb the path to acceptance ✻ if you can
warrior your spirit ✻ jump & hallelujah ✻ find place & mark
x ✻ know a body is something you have ✻ not something
you are ✻ try to sleep ✻ soundly ✻ without fear ✻ keep your
zest alive ✻ & do not forget ✻ which body you see through

Self-Portrait as Riddick

attempting to hide | who you are | is
beyond pointless | as your body | will always |
convict you | i swear this statement | is true |
do you like my eyes | their glow | got
em for a song | a pack of smokes | naturally |
forget | who you were & move | forward | got to
get off this planet | to a kinder one | & hope
help comes | but it doesn't | never does | & so
it's up to you | to make the plan | & execute |
joke's on them | you always had one | you always
knew how to get out | or at least | you knew you'd
learn how | given time | escape means | you
making a path | through the darkness | & the world's
nested threats | by any means necessary | getting
out | of whatever cuffs | or cage | or supermax
prison they put you in | it takes time | but you're no
quitter | sooner or later | you always get out | you're
renowned | for your escapes | in fact | but you can't
slip out of this one | so easy | like the rest | you are
trapped here | & have to find a way out | the rules are
upside down | & you're the expert | here | in survival |
viewing the terrain | & finding the road | reminds you |
we all hide | what we are | honestly | or go to some
extreme | to make it through | what the world throws down |
you keep | what you kill | you get me | for now | just
zap that next threat | & keep moving | through the black

Self-Portrait as Minority Report

abstractly ▲ I understand ▲ how the
body might ▲ be implicated ▲ in a
crime ▲ be its own crime ▲ to live
desaturated & cold ▲ is one destiny ▲ can be
essential ▲ to survival ▲ but it's hardly
fulfilling ▲ no way to live ▲ drowning ▲ in
guilt ▲ feelings of failure ▲ we are just as
human as you ▲ sometimes ▲ in a mirror ▲ my
irises shine ▲ & turn a particular shade of
jade ▲ if you didn't go looking ▲ you wouldn't
know ▲ it was there ▲ the green ▲ warm &
lively ▲ & I love these eyes ▲ this body ▲
my mother gave it to me ▲ it's everyone else
not seeing it ▲ or seeing it ▲ wrongly ▲
obfuscated ▲ echo ▲ laid over itself ▲ double
perception of what I ▲ am ▲ every glance cuts to the
quick ▲ you can only hide for so long ▲ everybody
runs ▲ wouldn't you ▲ if it was your body ▲ your
skin ▲ tender for their knives ▲ no matter what
title you may hold ▲ this is something I didn't use to
understand ▲ & now do ▲ & now I have no
vision of the future ▲ to trust ▲ & hold to ▲
weaponless ▲ I begin to understand ▲ to
-xins ▲ are everywhere ▲ so learn ▲ to accept
your inevitable fate ▲ it's a lose-lose scenario ▲ ha
-zards ▲ line the path ▲ but there is a way ▲ forward

Self-Portrait as *Fantastic Voyage*

advance cautiously ⌣ after all ⌣
bodies & brains ⌣ are delicate ⌣
caution ⌣ is key ⌣ if you want to
destroy ⌣ only ⌣ what you came for ⌣
every route requires ⌣ consideration ⌣
failure is not ⌣ an option ⌣ in this
game ⌣ of war ⌣ & so ⌣ you have to
hope you've ⌣ plotted carefully enough ⌣
indescribable things ⌣ around you ⌣ a
journey ⌣ fraught with peril ⌣ & you
know ⌣ you are haunted ⌣ hunted ⌣ inside
lung ⌣ & eye ⌣ through veins ⌣ into the
mind ⌣ where your target is ⌣ where
neurological processes ⌣ begin ⌣ & end ⌣
or are clotted ⌣ refusing to spark ⌣ to
properly adjust ⌣ the operation must be ⌣
quick ⌣ lasering away ⌣ every blockage ⌣
running on ⌣ bought time ⌣ betrayal
seems ⌣ inevitable ⌣ coming from within ⌣
too much damage done ⌣ from an impatient
urgency ⌣ to be done already ⌣ to finish
voyaging ⌣ traitors destroy themselves ⌣
white cells ⌣ end threats ⌣ easily ⌣ like a
xerox ⌣ flatten & shrink ⌣ inward ⌣
yawn around ⌣ the danger ⌣ then sail ⌣
zealously onward ⌣ & out ⌣ in tears ⌣ we save ourselves

Self-Portrait as Ragdoll 9

after the end ∴ of the world ∴ but
before we knew ∴ how to save individuals ∴
come together ∴ group ourselves safe ∴ we
discovered ∴ the beings that would be ∴ our
end ∴ crafted with ∴ precision ∴ exquisite
fine lines ∴ & elegant motion ∴ as they came ∴ no
grace extended ∴ no mercy ∴ animal ∴ that end
haunts us ∴ we had always known ∴ we were not ∴
invincible ∴ but we had to learn ∴ to be ∴
joyous in ∴ small victory ∴ we fought every
killer ∴ not with weapons ∴ but with a library ∴
learning ∴ how to best them ∴ in the end ∴ no
man survives ∴ or holds his whole soul ∴ alone
no single ∴ person can ∴ we know ∴ while the
one may be ∴ important ∴ they are not the only
person ∴ here ∴ & we all matter ∴ just as much ∴
quiet is all we have ∴ no music ∴ no chatter ∴ no
radio ∴ to signal ∴ our presence ∴ we need
silence to keep ∴ ourselves safe ∴ too much
talk ∴ too loud ∴ exposes us ∴ from where we hide ∴
underground ∴ but to live & find a voice ∴ is enough of a
victory ∴ after all ∴ even now ∴ at the end of the world ∴
we look out ∴ at the sky & its noxious fumes ∴ through
xenon ∴ & carbon ∴ invisible ∴ present ∴ & can say
yes ∴ we are still here ∴ yes ∴ if not all of us ∴ we zig &
zag between ∴ shelters ∴ yes ∴ but together ∴ we survive

Self-Portrait as *Pacific Rim*

adaptability ↀ has always been an asset ↀ
building ourselves ↀ new bodies ↀ new strength ↀ
cherno coyote crimson corinthian chrome
danger ↀ the names we give ourselves ↀ matter ↀ
exoskeletons ↀ are strong as ↀ we make them ↀ
fighting unwinnable wars ↀ every apocalypse more
grim than the last ↀ we think of ourselves ↀ as beyond
human ↀ we already see a body ↀ as something bigger ↀ
its bounds expanded ↀ its edges ours ↀ even if it's not a
Jaeger ↀ we don't see other people driving ↀ we see cars ↀ
Kaiju aren't the only monsters ↀ rising ↀ all of the pacific
language ↀ in the world won't stop them ↀ for that ↀ you
make weapons ↀ out of bodies ↀ the corps ↀ

newly created ↀ to fight back ↀ you learn ↀ how to un-
obstruct your mind ↀ let yourself be some ↀ oyster shell
pried open ↀ remade ↀ all pearls ↀ feel sea ↀ earth
quake ↀ when you make landfall ↀ a force of nature ↀ
resplendent ↀ something you can fight a hurricane in ↀ now
strike ↀ & eureka ↀ you've won the battle ↀ restart the
ticking clock ↀ this is a war of categories ↀ we constantly
undermine ourselves ↀ each rainy day we fear we'll never be
victorious ↀ fighting is exhausting ↀ everything is dark &
watery ↀ tides slamming you back ↀ to shore ↀ sometimes
xenowarfare means ↀ suiting up & becoming ↀ something
you never ↀ dreamed possible ↀ sometimes it means zero
zilch nada ↀ as there is no war ↀ no aliens here ↀ are there

Self-Portrait as Man in Black

aliens ■ exist ■ that is a fact ■ &
better yet ■ they walk among you ■
clothed unassumingly ■ blending in ■
diverse ■ as you could wish ■ or even
expect ■ in their bodies ■ they constantly
fake it ■ till they make it ■ that is ■ they
guess at what looks ■ normal ■ & act
how they think ■ normal acts ■ & if
incorrect ■ they will be spotted ■ by
J ■ whose whole name ■ is a letter ■ &
K ■ who shows him how ■ to make himself ■
lost in the crowd ■ letter a whole identity ■
make themselves ■ over again ■ until
nobody ■ can spot them ■ just like
outer space ■ beautiful ■ but background ■
people never ■ look up ■ your job is ■ to
quash rumors ■ allay suspicions ■ blend in ■
remove problems ■ your job is to become ■ a
suit ■ suited ■ to all situations ■ & to any
task ■ required of you ■ your job is to disappear ■
until you are tired ■ of hiding ■ you will not re-
veal yourself ■ until you are ready ■ so you
wait ■ for now ■ because you want ■ the real thing ■
xylitol is not sugar ■ lemonade is not water ■ you
yearn ■ to be recognized ■ & finally feel ■ the sharp
zing ■ of seeing yourself ■ triumphant ■ shining ■ bright

Self-Portrait as *Terminator*

always approach with care 💀 at first
because you don't know 💀 them yet
con artists 💀 are constant 💀 you might
decide they are 💀 safe 💀 only to find
evil 💀 looks human 💀 has a normal
face 💀 bleeds too 💀 the cruelest trick 💀
genuine care 💀 can't be faked 💀 that will
help you 💀 before you tell them 💀 name
identity 💀 origin 💀 give yourself away
just remember 💀 you are 💀 no hunter
killer 💀 you are a person 💀 trying to
live 💀 that's all 💀 counting every
minute 💀 carefully tracking 💀 each
new threat 💀 it's exhausting 💀 obviously 💀
observe 💀 your surroundings 💀 it's not
paranoia 💀 if they're really out to get you
question 💀 safety 💀 sanity 💀 evaluate
responses 💀 pick the best one 💀 keep yourself
safe 💀 at any cost 💀 & never stop
traveling across time 💀 till you get to a new
universe 💀 where you can look up 💀 let the
vibrant sun 💀 so different from huddled flames 💀
warm you through 💀 no models or types here 💀 no T-
Xes or T-800s or T-1000s 💀 just people 💀 living
yelling their joy 💀 fearless 💀 shining like steel 💀
zircon 💀 so bright 💀 so alive 💀 so human

Self-Portrait as Boba Fett

alone ⊤ is the best ⊤ way to be ⊤
bounty never comes ⊤ without work ⊤ building
character requires loss ⊤ the inevitable
disintegration ⊤ of the old ⊤ no need to
elide the self ⊤ if you never show it ⊤
face the world ⊤ opaque ⊤ & armored
grim & silent ⊤ gauntlet always on the
helm ⊤ in command of yourself ⊤ staying
implacable ⊤ things can be inescapable ⊤ even by
jetpack ⊤ but you can control yourself ⊤ use a
                kenning ⊤ instead of my name ⊤ make me
                lithograph ⊤ graven image ⊤ cast in steel ⊤
                Mandalorian ⊤ solo ⊤ this is how I want it
nod to acknowledge ⊤ never offer an
open hand ⊤ keep your face ⊤ your own ⊤ this
phenomenon is popular among our kind ⊤ keeping
quiet ⊤ as a defense mechanism ⊤ until the
reckoning ⊤ your metal edges become a
seismic shock ⊤ your body efficient ⊤ if
taciturn ⊤ you always get the job done ⊤
undertake any mission ⊤ you are not exactly
vicious ⊤ though you are vilified ⊤ the
words of others will not move you ⊤ you are
exactly ⊤ as resolute as you have learned to be ⊤
you are knocked back ⊤ but you fire a
zipline ⊤ & pull yourself ⊤ out of the pit

Self-Portrait as *Voyage Home*

absence is easy to define \ describe
bright to a person who's mired \ in night \ explain
cold to a desert dweller \ it's not so
difficult \ to recognize when you lack \ a thing
everyone seems \ to possess \ when that
facet \ seems fact \ something easy to
grasp \ don't misunderstand \ this existence is
hardly hardship \ just impossible \ to
imagine if it isn't \ yours \ it's in-
justice \ to demand the being \ changes \ an un-
kindness \ for it to reshape \ its nature
loss \ is easy to place \ & never minimal \ or
microscopic \ it radiates \ through future \ &
now \ we see its effects \ vast \ heaving \ like
ocean \ big as whalesong \ resonant \ some
planet itself \ waves of song \ & then a
quiet \ which is worse \ & also \
resonant \ how do we answer the absence \ its
song \ when we do not \ speak its language \
this is a problem no \ time travel will solve \
unless \ it will \ we find what we can \ share \
vibrations subtle \ & humming under
water \ a mistake to look for answers \ in
xenolinguistics \ as all along \ it was in
your body \ under your tongue \ it's
zero hour \ but you've brought it here

End Notes

Prior Publication

- "Self-Portrait as Space Odyssey" first appeared in OCEANS & TIME, an online blog published by *honey&lime lit*.

- "Self-Portrait as *Moon*" first appeared in *Moonchild Magazine*.

- "Self-Portrait as *Pacific Rim*" and "Self-Portrait as Riddick" first appeared in *Freezeray Poetry*.

- "Self-Portrait as *Avatar*," "Self-Portrait as Replicant," and "Self-Portrait as Thing" first appeared in *Prismatica Magazine*.

Acknowledgements

I'd like to thank all of my students in the NAPS Poetry Club—this all started with a poem prompt I gave to you, and your enthusiasm made me think continuing with the form was a good idea. I'd also like to thank everyone at the Providence Poetry Slam who loved these poems when I read them in open mics and made sure to tell me so.

Emily, Ethan, Fayce, and Max: thank you for helping me fine-tune these poems and make them better, and to all my poet friends on Twitter, thank you for sharing and exclaiming over the poems! You're all pearls and you make me a better writer and person. To my parents and Gwen, thank you for introducing me to these movies and fostering my love of science fiction.

I am grateful to every editor who published individual poems from this collection, and to *Vegetarian Alcoholic Press* for publishing the whole chapbook even after I incorrectly referred to them in my cover email (a mistake I still haven't quite recovered from).

I especially want to thank Victor for walking this road of discovery alongside me—I couldn't ask for a better copilot to sync with—and Damiana, my Drift partner, who so clearly understands how my brain works. Having both of you encourage both my poetry and my personal journey has meant the world, and helped me put my poetry and my self out there to be visible. I am so grateful to know you.

Symbols Glossary

/ — *Alien* —slashes left by xenomorphs
∞ — *Arrival* — time is an endless loop, what's past is future
🌿 — Dr. Ellie Sattler — paleobotanist
♪ — *Soylent Green* — final symphony
<< — *Planet of the Apes* — looking backward more than forward
% — *New Hope* — binary sunset
◎ — *TRON* — identity disc
▯ — *Matrix* — bullet time
¿ — *Thing* — who has been replaced?
{} — *Blob* — the shape of the Blob
>< — *GATTACA* — the double helix of a DNA strand
Ω — *Jupiter Ascending* — first and last Abrasax
≠ — Replicant — not equal
○ — *Moon* — the appearance of the Moon
[] — *Space Odyssey* — the shape of the monolith
() — Body Snatcher — the shape of the pods
⁂ — *Avatar* — the seeds of Eywa
| — Riddick — prison bars
▲ — *Minority Report* — the trio of precogs, the information blackout
⌣ — *Fantastic Voyage* — the shape of an eye, the spaces between
∴ — Ragdoll 9 — a fraction of 9
◍ — *Pacific Rim* — left and right hemispheres
■ — Man in Black — utilitarian, black, unobtrusive
☠ — *Terminator* — the machine
╦ — Boba Fett — the helmet visor
\ — *Voyage Home* — reverse of first poem, "backwards" time travel

Gretchen Rockwell is a queer poet currently living in Scotland for graduate studies. Xe is the author of two microchapbooks; xer work has most recently appeared in perhappened mag, Whale Road Review, Poet Lore, FreezeRay Poetry, and elsewhere. Gretchen enjoys writing about gender, history, myth, science, space, and unusual connections – find xer at www.gretchenrockwell.com or on Twitter at @daft_rockwell.